The adventures of Alice in Wonderland

Written and illustrated by Anne & Ken McKie
Published by
GRANDREAMS LIMITED,
Jadwin House, 205/211 Kentish Town Road, London NW5 2JU
Printed in Spain. ISBN 0 86227 329 3

One very warm summer afternoon, a little girl named Alice was sitting on a grassy bank, listening to her sister reading. Now Alice was feeling rather drowsy and just about to close her eyes for a moment when suddenly, a White Rabbit scampered by.

There was nothing really unusual about this — except that the rabbit was pulling a watch out of his waistcoat pocket . . . and talking to himself. "Oh dear! Oh dear! I'm late! I'm late!" he panted, as he scurried across the field.

Alice jumped to her feet and ran after him. She was just in time to see him dive into an enormous rabbit-hole and vanish. Without a second thought, Alice popped into the hole after that curious White Rabbit.

Once inside, the little girl felt herself falling quite slowly down what seemed to be a very deep well. As she floated towards the bottom, Alice noticed that shelves filled with books lined the sides. She passed tables and chairs, even mirrors and paintings; until she landed with a gentle thump on a pile of dry leaves.

She was just in time to see the White Rabbit running down a long passage. He was still looking at his watch, and still crying, "Oh my ears and whiskers how late it's getting!" Alice chased after him, but when she turned the corner he was gone.

Alice found herself in a long low hall. There were doors all around, she tried every one, but they were all locked. Suddenly, she noticed a little table made of glass, and on the top was a golden key. Behind the table Alice discovered a curtain — and behind the curtain, a very small door. She tried the golden key which, to her great delight, unlocked the door.

She knelt down and looked into the loveliest garden you ever saw. Alice sighed, "How I wish I was small enough to get through that door." She glanced back at the glass table — there on top stood a bottle (which certainly had not been there before). Tied round the neck was a label with "DRINK ME" printed on it in large letters.

Alice wisely checked that it was not marked "poison" and then she took a sip. It had a mixed flavour of cherry tart, custard, pineapple, roast turkey, toffee and hot buttered toast. "What a curious feeling," cried Alice, as she felt herself shrinking. "I must be shutting up like a telescope." She shrank so much that she was soon small enough to slip through the tiny door into the garden. But the silly girl had left the golden key on the glass table. And now she was so tiny, she couldn't reach it.

However, under the table was a glass box. In it was a small cake with the words "EAT ME" spelled out in currants. Alice gobbled up the cake and began to grow so large, her head hit the ceiling with a bang. "Oh dear!" sobbed Alice,bursting into tears. "Now I shall never get through that door." Her tears were so large they were like a flood. Soon, the whole room was knee-deep in water.

The sound of pattering feet made Alice dry her eyes. It was the White Rabbit. The sight of the giant Alice startled him so much that he dropped the gloves and fan he was carrying. Alice picked them up and realised she was shrinking again. She shrank so quickly, her feet slipped, and she fell into the deep pool made by her own tears.

"I wish I hadn't cried so much," said Alice, as she swam around in the salt water. In a little while she was joined by a mouse, who was just the same size as her. Soon the pool became quite crowded, as some very strange creatures and birds jumped in.

A big wave washed everyone up onto a beach. What a queer-looking party they were; there was a duck, a dodo, a lory and an eaglet, a crab, a magpie and a canary.

The dodo insisted on everyone joining in a Caucus-race. The silly creatures had no idea how to race properly. They just ran around in circles for half an hour, then shouted for prizes. Alice gave them a silver thimble from her pocket. And for a treat, she shared out a box of sweets among them.

In a little while, the White Rabbit came trotting by. Alice heard him muttering to himself. ''The Duchess! The Duchess! Oh my fur and whiskers! She'll have me executed. Where can I have dropped them?''

The White Rabbit looked up and noticed Alice for the first time. ''Run home this minute and fetch my gloves and fan,'' he called in a cross voice. Alice giggled. ''He thinks I'm the housemaid.'' So off she went and soon came upon a neat little house. It said ''W.RABBIT'' on a plate on the door.

She ran upstairs and found her way into a tiny bedroom. There on the dressing table was a fan, several pairs of gloves and a bottle. ''I'm tired of being tiny,'' said Alice. ''I'll drink it and see what happens.''

No sooner had Alice swallowed a mouthful than she grew and grew. She found her head was pressing against the ceiling — even if she lay down on the floor. "What on earth am I going to do?" cried poor Alice, putting one arm out of the window and one foot up the chimney.

Presently, the White Rabbit arrived calling for his gloves and fan. But try as he may he couldn't get into his house because it was full of Alice!

The White Rabbit was in such a state. He called his animal friends to help remove the monstrous Alice. She could hear the animals clambering on the roof and trying to get down the chimney. "We will have to burn the house down," shrieked the White Rabbit.

That was too much for Alice and she yelled back, "I shall set my cat on you if you do!" That did the trick. The animals ran a little way off and started to pelt things at the windows. "Now they're throwing little cakes," laughed Alice, as she caught one and bit into it. As soon as she swallowed the first mouthful she found herself shrinking again, until she ended up tiny once more.

Quickly she crept out of the White Rabbit's house and ran as hard as she could into the thick wood nearby. "Oh my goodness," squeaked Alice in a tiny voice, "I must find something magic to eat or drink. That seems the only way to get back to my right size."

Alice looked round her at the gigantic flowers and blades of grass. How tiny she felt. She stretched up on tiptoe and peeped over the edge of a mushroom growing close by. What a scare she got. Peering back at her was a blue caterpillar smoking a funny-looking pipe.

The caterpillar stared at Alice. ''Who are you?'' he demanded, puffing smoke into her face. Alice replied, rather shyly, ''I am Alice, but since I got up this morning I have changed so many times — I really don't know myself. And now I've ended up just so high.''

''That's the perfect height to be,'' said the caterpillar, as he puffed more smoke around. ''I am exactly the same height and I find that quite perfect.'' As the caterpillar got off the mushroom and crawled away, he shouted some advice to Alice. ''One side of the mushroom will make you grow taller — the other side will make you grow shorter.''

''Tell me which side?'' pleaded Alice. But the caterpillar had already disappeared. Quickly the little girl broke off a piece of mushroom with each hand. She nibbled the right hand piece and — whoosh — she grew so tall her head towered above the trees.

Alice began to panic. She nibbled first one piece of mushroom and then the other . . . sometimes growing taller, sometimes shorter. Until at last she brought herself down to a reasonable height although she was still very small. ''This size will do nicely,'' smiled Alice.

All at once she spied a little house in a clearing through the trees. "I wonder who lives in there?" she cried.

While she stood gazing at the house, the queerest thing happened. A fish dressed as a footman ran out of the wood and hammered on the front door. It was opened by a frog also dressed as a footman. The fish-footman bowed low to the frog-footman, and presented him with a big envelope. "From the Queen! An invitation to play croquet." They both bowed again and their curly white wigs got tangled up together.

Alice laughed so much she had to hide behind a tree. When she peeped out the fish-footman had vanished, and the frog-footman was left sitting on the doorstep.

Coming from inside the house, Alice could hear a great deal of howling, sneezing and loud crashing sounds. At this moment the front door opened, and a large plate came skimming out — hitting the poor frog-footman on the head.

Overcome with curiosity, Alice slipped inside the door. It led to a kitchen full of smoke from one end to the other. A cook was stirring a cauldron full of soup, and a Duchess was sitting on a stool nursing a howling baby. "There's certainly too much pepper in that soup," sneezed Alice. This made the cook so cross, she shook more and more pepper everywhere.

The Duchess was sneezing, Alice was sneezing, the baby was sneezing and howling both at the same time (which Alice thought was rather clever.) The only creatures not sneezing were the cook and a large cat, which was sitting on the hearth grinning from ear to ear. "Tell me," said Alice to the Duchess, "why does your cat grin so?"

"Because it is a Cheshire Cat," the Duchess yelled back, tossing the baby up and down until it howled louder than ever.

The cook took the soup off the stove, and began throwing everything within her reach at the Duchess. Saucepans, fire-irons, dishes and plates whizzed through the air. "Mind the baby's nose," cried Alice, terrified. "Here! You may nurse the baby if you like," yelled the Duchess. And she tossed the poor thing across the room towards Alice. "I must get ready to play croquet with the Queen."

Luckily Alice caught the baby and rushed outside to escape from all that pepper. "Stop grunting," said Alice, rather sharply to the baby. "It's very rude." But the baby snorted and kicked so hard that Alice put it down on the grass. To her great shock, the baby turned into a PIG, which trotted happily away into the wood.

"What a strange place this is," sighed Alice, "and which way do I go from here?"

"Depends on where you want to get to," came a voice from high up in a tree.

Alice looked up and was very startled to see the Cheshire Cat purring and grinning and showing a great many teeth. "In that direction," the Cat said, waving its right paw, "lives a Mad Hatter. And in that direction," waving his left paw, " lives a March Hare." The Cheshire Cat began to fade away, beginning with his tail, until only his grin was left. "A grin without a cat," thought Alice, "is the most curious thing I ever saw in my life."

She had not gone very far before she discovered the strangest house. The chimneys were shaped like ears and the roof was thatched with fur. "This must belong to the March Hare," laughed Alice. A large table was set out under a tree in the garden. The Mad Hatter and the March Hare were sitting crowded together at one corner of the table, having tea. Squashed in between them was a dormouse — fast asleep.

"No room! No room!" they both cried when they saw Alice coming.

"There's plenty of room!" said Alice crossly.

"Your hair wants cutting," said the Mad Hatter, peering at Alice.

"You should learn not to make such rude remarks," Alice snapped back. Then the March Hare and the Mad Hatter began to ask her silly riddles and such stupid questions that Alice could not make them out at all.

“What day of the month is it?” asked the Mad Hatter, shaking his pocket-watch. What a shock Alice got when he dipped it in his tea-cup. Then the silly pair poured hot tea onto the dormouse’s nose — just to wake him up. This is one of the funny poems the Mad Hatter told to Alice:

“Twinkle, twinkle, little bat!
How I wonder what you’re at!
Up above the world you fly,
Like a tea-tray in the sky.”

The last thing Alice saw when she decided to leave the crazy tea-party, was the Mad Hatter and the March Hare trying to put the sleeping dormouse into the tea-pot.

Once more Alice found herself in the long hall. There was the tiny glass table with the golden key on top. As she was still quite small, Alice could at last unlock the door and slip into the beautiful garden beyond.

A large rose bush stood near the entrance of the garden. The roses growing on it were white. However, there were three gardeners (who looked remarkably like playing cards) busy painting the roses red. Alice, of course, just had to find out why!

"We put a white rose bush in by mistake. The Queen only likes red." The poor gardener trembled as he spoke. "If she finds out she will cut off our heads."

Suddenly, all the gardeners fell flat on their faces. "The Queen! The Queen!" Marching into the garden came a huge procession of soldiers, courtiers and guests — all dressed like playing cards. The White Rabbit was there, followed by the Knave of Hearts, and last of all . . . the King and Queen of Hearts.

When the procession came level with Alice, the Queen stopped dead and bellowed. "What is your name, child?" Alice answered most politely. She was not a bit afraid (because after all, they were only a pack of playing cards.)

"And who are you?" screamed the Queen, pointing to the gardeners. "Off with their heads!" Alice began to argue, but the Queen kept shouting, "Off with their heads!"

“You shan’t be beheaded,” Alice promised the gardeners. And she hid them in large flower pots.

“Do you play croquet?” roared the Queen. As soon as Alice said she did, people began to run about in all directions. They were eager to get the game started before the Queen beheaded them all.

What a croquet game followed! The balls were live hedgehogs, the mallets live flamingoes, and the soldiers had to bend double to form the arches. The players all played at once, without waiting their turn. They quarrelled and fought, until the Queen was quite hoarse with shouting, “Off with their heads!”

Alice looked up to the sky in despair. There was the Cheshire Cat, (only his head, mind you) grinning down on the lot of them. "Off with his head!" shouted the Queen, as soon as she saw the cat's face. And the King himself hurried off to fetch the executioner.

What an argument followed! The executioner couldn't cut off the cat's head — because there wasn't a body to cut it off from. But the Queen kept insisting he did. "That cat belongs to the Duchess," announced Alice. "You'd better ask her about it." By the time the Duchess arrived, the Cheshire Cat's head had faded slowly away — and was gone.

As the game of croquet continued, so did the quarrelling. Soon, the Queen had everyone arrested until there was no-one left to play.

The Queen stopped, quite out of breath. "Have you met the Mock Turtle yet?" Alice had never heard of one, let alone seen one. Alice and the Queen walked off together and soon came upon a creature known as a gryphon. "Take this young lady to see the Mock Turtle!" ordered the Queen, as she marched off.

What a tale of woe Alice was to hear, told by the unhappiest creature she had ever seen. The Mock Turtle sang such sad songs by the sea-shore, that Alice was quite dismayed. He taught Alice a strange dance he knew. Even this did nothing to cheer him up. It was called the Lobster Quadrille and these are some of the accompanying words.

"Will you walk a little faster?" said a whiting to a snail.
"There's a porpoise close behind us, and he's treading on my tail.
See how eagerly the lobsters and the turtles all advance!
They are waiting on the shingle — will you come and join the dance?
Will you, won't you, will you, won't you, will you join the dance?
Will you, won't you, will you, won't you, will you join the dance?"

Alice heard a voice far away in the distance crying: "The trial is beginning." Without waiting to hear the end of the Mock Turtle's song, she ran away — leaving the poor creature still singing and sobbing on the sea-shore.

The King and Queen were seated on their thrones when Alice arrived (the King had a crown on top of a judge's wig). The court was full of little birds and beasts. A dish of tarts was on a table in the middle of the floor. And the poor Knave of Hearts was standing in chains looking very miserable.

The White Rabbit was there, looking most important with a parchment scroll and a trumpet. "Silence in court!" he cried, and blew three blasts on his trumpet.

''The Queen of Hearts, she made some tarts,
All on a summer's day;
The Knave of Hearts, he stole those tarts,
And took them quite away!''

''First witness,'' called the White Rabbit. It was the Mad Hatter still carrying his cup of tea and a slice of bread and butter. He was far too frightened to make much sense.

The next witness was the cook. She carried her pepperpot with her and made everyone in court sneeze. ''What are tarts made of?'' asked the King. ''Pepper mostly!'' replied the cook. The dormouse interrupted and was promptly thrown out. During all this confusion — Alice seemed to be growing bigger.

Imagine her surprise when she was called as the next witness. Alice jumped up, quite forgetting how large she had grown in the last few minutes. The edge of her skirt caught the jury-box, and she tipped all the animals and birds out onto the floor.

The court was in uproar. The King called out: "All persons more than a mile high to leave the court!" Everyone looked up at Alice accusingly.

"You're nearly two miles high!" screamed the Queen. It was quite clear to Alice that the Knave of Hearts was not getting a fair trial. "This is stuff and nonsense!" cried Alice.

"Hold your tongue!" yelled the Queen, turning purple. "Off with her head." But nobody moved.

"Who cares for you?" said Alice (she had grown to full size by now). "You're nothing but a pack of cards!"

At this, the whole pack rose up into the air, and came flying down on her. Alice gave a little scream, half of fright and half of anger. She tried to beat them off, and found herself lying on a grassy bank. Dried leaves had fluttered down from the trees on to her face. Her sister was gently brushing them away.

"Wake up, Alice," said her sister. "Why, what a long sleep you've had!"

"I've had such a curious dream!" said Alice. "Well, at least I think it was a dream . . ."